Book I in the Legacy Series

The Legacy Awakens
"Outpouring"

Danny Williams

The Legacy Awakens-Outpouring
Copyright © 2021 by Danny Williams

ISBN 978-1-7377883-3-1

Printed in USA
Published by SIP Publications, LLC & Junior Authors
Cover Design by 5:13 Graphics & Media, LLC

Dedication

I'm dedicating my first book to my mom. She always encourages me to pursue my dreams. I love writing and now it's happening! I thank you so much for believing in me. All your love, support, and hard work have been noticed. I appreciate all that you do!

Table of Contents

Prologue

It was all because of him. His creators, blinded by greed and malice, made a horrible mistake. A mistake called…him. The thought caused a smirk to spread across his face. They had brought this on themselves. They had tried to control something far beyond their knowledge. He knew they called him evil. He didn't care. After all, he was living proof of their hypocrisy, born of their vile emotions, their evil intentions. Their experiments and their tests, all for the sake of *using* him, birthing a weapon to better kill their kind. Their words meant nothing. They had toyed with him, so he would do the same. They'd hoped the energy born of their kind's vileness would be a spark to light their futures. Instead, he set their world ablaze. Inside his anarchic mind, he felt many different things, as he thought about what had led to this moment. Guilt was the one he felt least. With such flawed Kings, such irrational people, there was no way they could have avoided their fate. War had been inevitable. All he'd done was tip the scales a little. And now he'd just sit back and watch the fireworks.

"For the last time, the answer's no." The king's voice was thick with exasperation as if this was a topic he'd long since exhausted his patience on. The man he was speaking to sat nearby in a chair, expression filled with bitterness and barely tempered fury.

"And yet again, *your majesty,* I *must* request you to hear. *Me. Out.* You *never do,* after all. It's difficult to do my job with a king *too blind* to see what's staring him in the face." The king flushed with rage.

"You dare think you have the right to speak to me that way? Even if you're my chief advisor, **I am your King!**"

"A king blinded by his inability to think rationally! They may be your ally now, but only a fool doesn't take measures to ensure his future!" The king's veins were practically bulging out of his forehead.

"**Measures like creating a weapon to attack our own allies. Like experimenting with power, we can't even fathom?**"

"That's not for *you* to think about! That's what our scientists are for!"
At this, the king's face took a slightly more…dangerous look. A scowl spread across his face.

"*Indeed,* that is what our scientists are for. But given their *utter failure* to harness it in their *last* experiment, the one you authorized 'behind my back.'-" The advisor's face paled.

"Y-you *know* about that. B-but I thought -"

"That you'd scrubbed the records, yes. Trust me, I'm aware, despite what you believed. That was such a shame, too. So many talented scientists, gone so fast. And the poor fool who *tested it*…no doubt you still have him sealed away somewhere, correct?"

"Sir, I-I-I've only done what I think is best for this kingdom!"

"I'm sure, which is also why you've been in contact with some of the nation's most famous scientists. Famous for being criminals and *murderers!* You committed *treason,* just like them."

"E-Even if they've betrayed this kingdom, at least they have the vision to know it needs defending from those egotistical fools, those-those savages hiding behind a façade of order and logic!" He closed his mouth in an instant, but it was too late. Revulsion and understanding instantly crept along the king's face.

"…***Ahh. I see.***"

"*Y-your majesty, I-I didn't mean-*"

"And so, you finally reveal your true colors. This was *never* about the escalating tension in Kosaint, was it? It was about *you.*" Anger colored the advisor's face.

"How dare you accuse me of selfishness! All I've done for you, for this *kingdom!* You and I **both** know they don't respect us; they don't like us; they're *amused* by us. I've already heard rumors that their

King is plotting to betray us! His servants don't trust us, after all. We need to strike first!"

"Enough! I have ignored your treachery long enough. The darkness in a heart like yours only further proves the folly of trying to weaponize such a thing. Guards!" At his yell, several men swarmed the area. The advisor tried to flee but was stopped in his tracks. "Arrest this man…for treason."

As the man was dragged away shrieking, small tears streamed down his face, he yelled in fury,

"You'll see! You'll be sorry for what you've done today. I only wanted to save your kingdom from its fate. But now you'll just have to wait until it falls apart at the hands of your 'friends."

And with that, he was dragged away to be imprisoned. As they trudged toward his future prison, he stewed. He thought about all the times he'd tried to warn the king, all the sacrifices he'd made for *his* sake, his *stupid kingdom's* sake. All he'd wanted was to protect his home from those who could destroy it. **Who would,** he reminded himself. With a military that strong, a country that strict and loyal, it was only a matter of time, he was *sure* of it. If that foolish king had just listened to him…perhaps they could have avoided such a fate. But it was too late now. He was on his way to the place he'd spend the rest of his life. At least, until he saw an explosion out the corner of his eye, and saw several guards fall. Out of the commotion came several of the scientists he'd hired, complete with gear, one of which came over to him, helping him up from the ground.

"Good to see *you're* doing well."

"I could say the same. Safe to say the king is *not* on board with your plan?"

A small smile crossed his face. "Yep."

"So, we're still doing it?"

"Yep."

"You do realize that attempting to weaponize energy made from the worst parts of humanity can *only* backfire, right?"

"Yet to be seen, but kinda."

"We'll probably die."

"If it works, it's worth it."

"So, this is basically mad science?"

"Mad science." The scientist's face practically beamed. "My favorite."

That smile admittedly made him uneasy. For a moment, he questioned the choices he'd made. The hand he'd chosen. He shook his head. Too late for doubts now. All he could do was succeed. His smile grew. He'd show that stupid king. He'd make him realize just how right he was. He'd save their kingdom. And when their kingdom was safe…they'd have the "criminal advisor" to thank.

Chapter One

She was seeing the image again. A girl stumbling into the wilderness, the firing of bows and slices of swords not far behind her. How long had she been seeing this? Weeks? Months? Her skull was pounding. Time always seemed to blur together when the visions happened. It didn't matter. It never did. Tears still always flowed down her cheeks at the sight of the fallen, the bloody remains of their hopes and dreams. She didn't understand. Why did this keep happening? They'd told her it would stop, that she was fine. A lie she believed less and less by the second. As she watched the girl scream at phantoms that weren't there, feeling as though she wanted to scream, too. Was she going mad? The thought was terrifying. What terrified her more was the fact that the more this happened, the more she felt that she knew the uniforms, knew the girl shrieking into the night. The more she realized that this was the thing she feared most. She didn't want to think about this. She didn't want to keep seeing this. She just wanted it to stop. The screams of pain and clashes of iron continued to echo long after the visions passed.

Why was this still happening? A grim expression overshadowed his face. The doctor had said it was a phase. That it would stop. And yet here he was, listening to her whimpers from outside the door. An uncharacteristic moment of concern struck him. Perhaps it was time to reveal what he knew to her.

Despite the desire to tell her, he hesitated. He disliked her suffering, but was unwilling to sacrifice all that he'd done, all he'd worked for…even for her sake.

He journeyed down the hall from his daughters' room to his study. With a sigh he reached towards a small, locked cabinet near the end of the room. It was old, wood chipped, slight scratches across the glass. Nobody would have ever guessed the secrets it had contained. With a bone-chilling sense of foreboding, he pushed each of the numbers to the lock. Not another person alive knew them. Or ever would. With a slight groan, the lock fell off, and the two glass doors creaked open. Hands slightly shaking, he reached out, attempting to grasp the contents within. Gripping them, he carefully began to open the folder.

Within the folder were items he'd seen several times before. It contained a ravaged report detailing an argument between the Kings of Kalmte and Kosaint, a soldier's torn notebook full of insane rambling about beings who could dodge any strike and cripple entire armies, a mostly burnt documentation of an unofficial experiment with negative energy, and mud-stained letters between a king's advisor and history's most infamous scientists. The man didn't care about any of this. What he had wanted, he'd removed already. The writing was faded, the pages barely legible, the drawn images smeared, but even so, they represented some of the last pieces of evidence that Kina and all the people she'd saved had ever existed. Beloved keepsakes, of his wife. He left a single, insignificant page behind, just enough to connect to the rest.

Face showing hints of frustration and fear, he turned towards the warmth of his fireplace. Looking into the fiery depths of the blaze, he couldn't help but think of what awaited him for what he had done in life. He didn't care much about the opinions of men, of all those who had called him cruel and heartless. In this moment, however, he wondered if this was his final chance to turn back. To do what his daughter had so begged him to. He turned his head. No. It had cost him too much, *would* cost him too much. And even if he did…no. It was too late for him. Too late for doubts. This was who he was. He looked down, as if to stare the fireplace in the eyes. He grasped the papers tighter, as if they would fly away had he let go. He thought of the man he'd met. The man who'd reminded him of what he had become. A razor-thin smile crossed his face. At first, he'd felt a tad bitter towards him. And now, he couldn't help but thank him. Had it not been for him…had it not been for him… "I wouldn't have been able to do this now." And with that, he threw the papers into the inferno.

Chapter Two

She knew it was here. It *had* to be. It had been one mystery after another, things just weren't adding up. Her father kept hiding things, kept conversing with men, strange men she's never seen before, not to mention the strange questions he'd been asking lately. She'd have asked her mother, but it'd have been pointless. She hadn't left her room in what felt like years. She couldn't be relied on. *She never has been.* Suina rebuked the thought. Her mother loved her. It wasn't her fault. Wasn't her fault everything had happened. Wasn't her fault the mobs outside hated her, that it felt like the world was against her. It was her father's. Him and his secrets. That was why she had to do this. As her hands touched the thick wooden door, she hesitated. Once she opened this door it would never close for her. She'd have to find *something.* She'd be damaging her father's trust in her beyond repair.

There was still so much she wished to do, things that required his trust more than his honesty. She wasn't blind to the poverty-stricken workers with limited options and meager pay, the hatred and malice of the people outside who saw him as a greed-stricken fiend. She could change all that. But only if she didn't do this. She frowned. She'd have her regrets either way. She'd already made it this far. It was too late to think again. Inhaling deeply, she took the plunge and stepped inside. It had been years since she'd last stepped foot in this room, yet she moved as if she'd been there every day. She carefully maneuvered around the dim room, gently feeling around the nearby cabinets and desks. Her father's chair was turned towards the window, the way he always left it. A light switch was nearby. She didn't dare turn it on. All she needed was a clue, anything that would help her discover the truth. She was hoping that this little fishing expedition would land her something big, but she was taking a tremendous risk.

She inched her way along the wall, mind consumed with purpose. Suddenly she grew still as her hands connected with a small, locked cabinet. Her pulse raced in anticipation as she realized that she'd struck gold. This was it, she thought. No more secrets, no more mysteries. She thought she heard a slight sigh as she found the cabinet, one filled with disappointment and sadness, but she chalked it up to her nerves. She knew that she'd just crossed a line, and her father would be extremely mad if he found out what she was about to do. But at least she'd know what he was keeping from her. Her hand touched the lock, as she prepared to try and break it. Suddenly, the window in front of the room exploded. Small shards of shattered glass skimmed her arm, and the scent of fresh blood filled her nostrils. Out of the corner of her eye she spied a small round object next to a piece of paper. Knowing her time was up, she had to make a quick exit. She raced for the door, scooping the paper up as she made her way out. Her exit hadn't come a moment too soon. Her father's personal guards entered the room and closed the door behind them. She lingered in the hallway for a moment, trying to overhear the conversation the guards were having. She heard three voices. The third voice burst into the conversation, shaking with tranquil fury, and my heart stopped. She instantly recognized it as her father's.

"We have two problems. I want you two to take care of whoever threw that rock, and I...I'll take care of my daughter."

She had been out of the office mere seconds before the chair had turned, revealing the man that'd been facing the window.

"I knew she was curious," her father stated, "but that curiosity is becoming a problem. It's one thing for her to question me, it's another thing entirely to *disobey* me and *break into my files.*"

"Did she find out anything?"

"No...no, she didn't. I burnt the file she wanted a long while ago." As he said this, he made a slight gesture towards the fireplace. "And she didn't find anything else. That rock smashed through the window just in time. But I can't risk it. Even one of those files has the potential to bring down everything I've worked for, everything I've *earned.* I *won't* let her *ruin that.*"

One of the bodyguards appeared to tense up a bit at his words, at the tone behind them. A drop of sweat fell down his face.

"Why not just burn them too, then?" A small smile, gone as quick as it appeared.

"Because for all the danger they bring, they give me leverage beyond what I could imagine. Her *meddling* could ruin that."

"T-then, what are you gonna do, boss?" For a moment, silence. The question seemed to weigh on the man as if his very soul didn't like the answer. The moment of doubt ended as soon as it began, however, and the man rose to his feet with renewed determination in his eyes. "I once said that I'd do whatever I had to, even if she is my daughter. And I have every intention to keep my word…no matter what. As I said…I'll take care of her. It's my responsibility to do so."

She flinched back from the door at this, face practically pale with shock and fear. Wh-what she'd just heard…it…it *couldn't* be *true.* She-she *had* to have misheard it, *imagined it.* H-her father wouldn't-he *couldn't* have… "…**take care of me**?" What did he mean? Her father was not a man to make idle threats. In fact, he didn't *make* threats. Whatever he said, he **did**. If…if he said he was going to…to take care of her…then…*then*…No. *No.* This-this *couldn't be* **happening. NO.**

"H-he wouldn't-he-he…" And with that she slumped to the floor, tears flowing down her cheeks. It…it was just too much. Her father…she…she'd always known he wasn't a good person. That much had been clear. All the secrets, all the shady dealings, it was obvious. But even so…she'd…she'd thought he…loved her. At least enough not to do *this.* Thoughts and theories were racing through her head. How much was a lie? She thought about the doctor's visits, of the strange nightmares she'd had, of that weird memory of a flipped car. They'd said it was all normal, or luck, or that they would stop. Lies. She'd been lied to. That's all he'd been doing. Her head was practically spinning. She didn't know what was going on. She didn't know what to do. She was thinking of what to do when she heard her father say, "One of you needs to tell her mother of her unfortunate disappearance. I'm unsure if she'll care much, given her absence from the child's life lately, but the formality is necessary. We…we don't want her to make a scene. This needs to be…discreet. You tell her I want to talk to her about something. There is a secret I'm tired of keeping. Then go to the garden and prepare. Everyone else, talk to the security team, see if they were able to capture any of the people who broke my window." That was the boost she needed. The thing required to shock her out of the moment. It didn't matter *why* her father wanted her dead. It didn't matter what she didn't know. She'd figure it all out later. What she did know was that she had to leave, *now.*

She rushed to grab a few things from nearby rooms and took off running just as the door began to open. Momentarily looking behind her, she saw the guard's face open a little in shock, and she heard the words, "Hey, Suina, your father wants to talk-h-hey, stop that! Stop! She's running away! Stop her! Grab her!"

But it was too late. In an instant, she was turning the hallway corner, knowing she didn't have much time. Already she could hear more of her father's security reentering the building, hearing the order, and presumably giving chase. She saw the door less than 50 feet away but found a larger bodyguard giving chase...and reaching into his pocket for something black. She looked for somewhere to turn, to *run*, but found *nowhere*. As the shape took full clarity in her view, she tensed, knowing that this was the end of her journey. She thought about what she'd just thrown away. Her mother would be abandoned, left only with her pitiful excuse of a husband. Her father would have killed his only child, solely to protect his assets. She'd wasted her life, accomplished nothing, solely because she selfishly looked for answers. She wished she could start over. Do *more*. *Help someone.* But it was too late now. She closed her eyes, waited...heard the shot...nothing. Nothing. Behind her, she could hear one of the guards saying, "What in the-" before finally bursting out the door and taking off into the forest nearby, face streaked with sweat and hints of panic. Her mind was pure and utter chaos: what had just happened? She grabbed her arms, her shoulders, double-checking that she was, indeed, in one piece. After confirming that 1. She was safe and 2. Yes, that had just happened, she did the only rational thing and promptly freaked out.

At the house, however, her father was eerily calm as he heard the words, "She…she got away, sir." He calmly said, "Thank you for the update. Now go bring me the security footage, and the guard who fired on her." As the man left, the father calmly poured himself a glass of apple cider, took 3 sips, then proceeded to angrily throw the bottle into the fire. As the fire dimmed and choked, he regained some composure. By the time the guard and the footage were there, he was practically normal. The guard appeared tense, as he should be. "Please, sit down." Despite the "please," one got the feeling that this was *not* a request. Of course, the man sat, sweating bullets from every pore. The fellow across from him, on the other hand, still had his cool facade.

"Apologies. I intended for us to have apple cider together, but I, unfortunately, dropped the bottle." Timidly, the guard looked over at the dying fireplace, now littered with glass.

"N-no problem, boss. I wasn't thirsty."

"Good to hear. Now, if you don't mind, I have some questions for you." The guard's face was sheet pale.

"O-of course, boss."

"Thank you. To begin, I heard that after my daughter fled the building, you gave chase, correct?"

"Y-yes, sir. She was fast, but I managed to keep up with her."

"And yet she escaped."

"Y-yes, sir. I'm deeply sorry, I did everything I could to stop her."

"Indeed. Speaking of which, the strangest thing: a *bullet* was found at the scene. Seeing as you were the closest person to her, is it safe to assume that you were, of course, the person who fired it at her?"

"Y-yes, sir."

"That is, despite my *direct* order to let *me* handle how my daughter was dealt with?"

"I-I-"

"Fear not. I'm usually not a man of second chances, but today I'm feeling merciful. I'll overlook this transgression, given she's still alive. This will still carry quite the demotion, of course. We'll discuss *that* later, but this leads to my final question: if you fired on her from point-blank range, then why is she still alive? Furthermore, why is there no blood on the bullet? As a matter of fact, it appears *damaged, bent* even. Do you mind explaining to me how that is possible?" The guard responded through choked breaths.

"I-I don't-I must have mis seen-"

"I don't need your *excuses;* I need an answer. Did you simply miss a target less than 50 feet from you? If so, I see little reason to keep you employed in *any* form…"

"N-no, sir, no, sir."

"Then why?"

"I…I…I don't-" A sigh.

"I wished not to have to resort to such a method, but very well. Let's watch the footage, then."

And so, they did. They watched as the man pulled his gun, fired…and they couldn't believe their eyes. As she closed her eyes and the bullet traveled, the air right behind her appeared to gain the slightest green tinge…before the bullet bounced off the unstable, shattering field, and fell behind her, the evidence fully fading with the closing of the door. The guard's face was grim, as if he felt this condemned him rather than absolving him. After all, what he'd seen…it was impossible. The stuff of stories. The only reasonable explanation was sabotage. He was sure he'd be accused of trickery, sent to meet an untimely end. However, when he looked over, he was surprised. The man's face had grown calmer. He was downright *serene.* He simply turned off the T.V. and said, "I see. Well, you clearly did everything you could. You are free to leave. Please go see if they found the person who threw that rock. I wish to chat with him."

Gibbering random praises, the guard practically scrambled for the door, until he heard, in a bone-chilling voice,

"Oh, and one thing. If you tell *anyone* what you just saw, consider yourself, I mean your employment *terminated* without severance."

The thud heard as the door closed behind the guard could be heard throughout the entire house. Behind that door, a troubled father was sitting in his chair, thinking about how he'd just seen the impossible. He thought back to the journal he'd found, the one from long ago. The one that claimed incredible beings with unfathomable powers, who'd defeated the armies of two warring kingdoms at once. At first, he had thought it mostly fiction, or over-exaggeration. The ravings of a broken mind. After he'd received a visit from the guys in black and white, he found himself unsure. He'd known that whatever had happened back then, whatever was in these pages was the knowledge that would change everything. Hesitantly, he put in the code to his safe. There, he took out the small, torn notebook he'd been ignoring. He never thought the day would come where he'd truly read it. He thought it over, time and time again. But in the end, it wasn't really a choice. Slowly but carefully, not missing a single remaining scrap of detail, he began to read the words on the pages.

Chapter Three

After she had successfully stopped freaking out for a second, Suina decided it might be a good idea to stop and clear her head, given the circumstances. So, she stopped, and began to list what she knew so far:

1. She'd been having strange visions for the last few months of a woman in a war, one that looked familiar.
2. Her father was hiding something, something *important.*
3. His secrets were important enough that other people wanted them. *Badly.*
4. *Whatever* he was hiding, he was willing to *kill her* over it.
5. Somehow, she had utterly avoided getting shot from *point-blank range.*

…*not exactly* a lot to go off of. Absent-mindedly, she stuck her hands in her pockets, trying to think through what she knew. She wondered why she'd been given this second chance, the one she'd desired so much. Another chance to help those she cared about. Suddenly, she heard a rustling noise and felt paper sliding across her palm. Curious, she pulled out the object she'd felt. To her surprise, it was a letter of some sort. She suddenly remembered grabbing the paper in a panic as she'd rushed out of her father's office. It was most likely meant for him, and him alone. Obviously, this shouldn't have mattered at this point, but even so, she couldn't help but hesitate. Was it one last sign she still respected her father? Maybe so, but if it was, it was one she knew she couldn't afford to let stop her. She slowly uncrumpled the paper and began to read the contents.

"Hey, Suina. Yes, we know it's you reading this right now. Don't ask how, just know that we know. We also know your father's been lying to you. A lot. And you hate it. So let us fill you in a little: those dreams are *not* normal, for *multiple* reasons. Your father knows that, and that's why he's hiding it. Your fathers got more skeletons in his closet than a costume shop, and that little secret is just one of them. If things have gone the way we think, you're probably feeling alone right now. You have no idea where to go from here, no idea who to trust. You feel like there's nobody else who can get how you're feeling. But we do, we know how you feel because we've all been there. This may not seem all that comforting, given you're hearing this via creepy letter, but you can trust us. There's a *lot* of things we want to tell you, a lot of secrets to unravel…but we can't yet. In time, we promise.

The letter abruptly cut off, leaving her with more questions than answers. Who'd sent her this? Why'd they say she could trust them? *How* could she possibly trust them when they didn't even give her their names? How had they *known* she'd be the one reading this?

They'd thrown it through her *father's* window! So many questions went through her mind, none of which she had an answer. As she was trying to figure out where exactly to go from here, she spotted a shadow out the corner of her eye, darting around, closer, and closer. She tried to track it, but it was too fast for her, no matter where she tried to look. The next thing she knew, the shadow was right behind her, and she could hear a person's breathing a few feet away. Suddenly, she felt a hard strike on the back of her head and sprawled onto the ground. Ignoring the searing pain, she tried to look at her attacker. As she turned around, she saw a child a little older than her, looking a tad hesitant, but stern.

"Sorry, but I had to stop you from running. Relax, I don't intend to hurt you. Your father found me and asked me to give you a message." Her father? Why did he send this kid? And why was he bothering to send messages at this point?

"What does he want?"

"Your father has learned something quite interesting today, it seems. Interesting enough that he went out of his way to find me. He wants you back, to talk to personally. He promises that if you comply, he'll forget everything that happened today. Things will be better. If not…" He looked uncomfortable at that point. "…just comply, please. Make it easier on us both."

Understandably, she was hesitant to just give up and let her father decide her fate, after the events earlier.

"My father isn't the type to simply let things go. He never has been. Why now? What's so special about me?" Her assailant chuckled a little at this, hints of bitterness tainting the sound.

"Not sure, but best guess? You…are like me."

"What?"

"…You'll get it in time. For now, suffice to say, you're *much* more special than you think. Otherwise, we'd be having a rather different conversation. It's also why I'd appreciate it if you could just come quietly, and not make things difficult."

Now, *this* was interesting information. Her father wanted her back. No, he *needed* her for something. That's how it always was with him. Whether you were useful, or you weren't. And she was of use to him. She had to think about this. If she went back, she'd have leverage. She could try and get answers, answers he'd *have* to give. She'd finally have the truth…maybe. And even if she did, it would cost her. She had no idea what he would use her for, what of hers he even *wanted* to use. She'd still just be listening to whatever he told her like she'd done *her entire life.* She already knew what her answer would be.

"Sorry, but…no. I can't trust him. Not anymore." The child sighed heavily.

"Fair enough. Still…we both know I can't just let you go. He won't let me go back there without you. So…I guess I have to fight you." Well, *that* wasn't good.

"Um, *or* you could come with me!"

"Yeah, sorry, but no. I have someone I need to keep safe and making an enemy of the city's biggest corporation isn't doing that."

"Well, it was worth a shot."

"C'mon, get up. If I must do this, I'm not going to hit you while you're down."

How generous. Begrudgingly, Suina pulled herself to her feet, still nursing the hit from earlier. Seeing it, the opponent showed signs of guilt.

"Oh. Oh, yeah. Fine, then. I'll let you get one free hit in." Her feelings were conflicted, to say the least. Yes, she was annoyed at being hit, but she wasn't exactly the violent type. She didn't like to fight. She didn't know how to fight. And even if she did, she hated hurting people.

"I...I can't."

"Look, sorry, but we're doing this. Just hit me." With great reluctance, she balled up her fist and punched him square in the cheek. The person flinched a little but seemed to shake it off quickly. Suina, on the other hand, now had a sore hand she was nursing. She soon heard her foe talking. "Not bad, but I can tell you're not used to this. Still, time to just quit and come with me." The answer was swift.

"Nope."

"Well, I tried. Look, I'll give you a second head start. That's...the best I can do."

"Thank-"

"20, 19, 18, 17…" She quickly got the hint and got to running. While disappointed in how it had ended, she couldn't help but appreciate how many chances he'd given her. As she looked for somewhere in the thick trees to go, she heard him finish.

"…2,1,0. That's it, I can't keep stalling."

In an instant, she saw him darting through the thick trees, at a pace far too fast for a human, especially one his age. His face held a grim expression, but his movements were consistent, unrestrained. Suina's mouth practically dropped as he searched dozens of feet worth of bulky oaks in a matter of seconds. As he grew closer, she tried to step back, preparing to make a break for it. However, she stumbled as the back of her foot hit a fallen branch, and before she could right herself, he was there. He seemed to be getting more and more hesitant…and annoyed.

"C'mon, do something. If you're like me, now's the time to show it, because even if I hate it…we're done stalling." Now *she* was getting mildly annoyed.

"What exactly *are* you? How am I 'like you'? And why does my father want me back?" A little more hesitation.

"I wish I could tell you, but that's not how life is. You'll have to figure it all out."

And with that, he finally threw a punch. It was slow, restrained, but Suina still barely dodged it. He continued to throw halfhearted but strong punches, most blocked or dodged. As she fought with this person, she thought about if what she was doing was worth it. After all, she didn't know why her father was even doing this. Maybe he just wanted to make amends, in his own twisted way. Maybe she was wrong. Maybe she should go back to him. She thought about her mother, who she'd left behind alone to deal with her father. She felt guilt at how selfish she'd been. She even thought about the person she was fighting. It was obvious he had no choice in the matter. She oddly wanted to help him with his situation, despite knowing that it would cost her everything. She wanted the best for everyone involved, she struggled with it. She halfheartedly attempted to throw a punch back at the one fighting her, but was easily blocked, arm caught, wide open. She knew the fight was as good as done. Despite that, she felt an odd calm layering her fear and frustration. At least now, she knew they'd all get what they wanted. With her utterly cornered, he threw what would have been the final hit...if a light green barrier hadn't blocked it midway, cracking slightly from the force of the strike. The boy's face lit up, a twisted mix of shock and excitement.

"Uh...figure it out yet?"

Suina's eyes went wide. Her eyes went blank. She could only give a stunned nod. Her attacker smiled a little.

"Kinda cool, to be honest. If you come back to him, we can probably figure everything out. Together."

That shook her out of it. She was still confused at everything that was going on, but she quickly realized that whatever had just happened, whatever this was, *that* was what her father wanted her for. It wasn't love. It wasn't family. She was just another asset to him. Another tool. Anger flashed through her mind at her father. No, he didn't deserve that name. Her betrayer. As the green shield shattered just as he was about to end the fight, someone rammed into him from the side, knocking him several feet away…through a tree. Suina could've sworn she heard the words, "Sophia's gonna kill me for this." Then the person ran towards her, facing a grim mix of concern and an odd amusement. As she looked closer, she saw what it was: a boy in his mid-to-late teens, average in appearance except for the countless scratches, cuts, bruises, and scars that trailed down his neck, arms, and legs. His pants had several tears in them, each slightly stained with crimson. Even looking at him made her flinch. She could only imagine the things he'd seen; he'd dealt with. Even so, he seemed to carry himself with an air of determination, like he was already committed towards dealing with whatever fate threw at him. It was oddly reassuring.

"Well, sorry to interrupt your date, but given the circumstances, didn't think you'd mind." A small smile crept across Suina's face at this.

"It's fine. I don't think he was my type, anyway." Then the hints of humor she had vanished, as she started to put two and two together.

"You-are, you the one who sent that letter through the window?" Hesitation.

"Well, I can't really hide everything from you at this point, can I?" A sigh.

"Yes and no. I helped write it, but I wasn't the only one. We talked about how much to tell you...several times."

"Good to see you guys decided to put a lot of trust in me." The person snickered.

"Okay, that's fair, but give me a little credit, I advocated to fill you in on things. Besides..." His face darkened a bit. "It looks like we'll have to bring you into the fold anyway. We can't exactly allow your father to have you, not now that he seems to have caught on." Suina was about to ask for detail when they both heard a pained groan from behind the fallen tree. A hand grasped its trunk, and the person's crimson-streaked face emerged from behind, annoyance obvious.

"Stay out of this! This is none of your business!"

Slight shock crept across Suina's face. She hadn't really thought about it, but he'd just slammed clean through a tree, after flying 20 feet, with only bruises to show. That must have been what he meant by being "like her." Her rescuer's face darkened further.

"I think you should stay with us. You'll get all your answers." This offer sounded strangely familiar.

"My father gave me a similar offer. And just as much info. How do I know you guys won't use me like he wanted to?" The boy's face gained a dark, slightly bitter smile.

"Because to be honest, my partner probably doesn't even want you with us. Not yet. This was kind of...unauthorized. And besides..." He looked as the fallen child slowly rose. "...you're a little low on options."

Suina thought deeply on the matter, considering the options. She was about to respond when she heard, "Hey, look out!" and turned to see a kick heading right for her. She blocked, but the force still sent her sprawling, and her head collided with a nearby tree. Her vision went white. She vaguely saw her rescuer kick the attacker away, before turning to her. The last thing she heard before she faded away was, "Oh, this is going to be *fun* to explain."

Chapter Four

She woke up with a starry sky in her sight. Taking a moment, the dazed girl tried to clear her head. She blinked and found that the voice of the person who'd rescued her was now accompanied by another.

"It wasn't wise to risk your safety to save her, and even less wise to bring her *here.* We can't afford another person."

"Another *kid.* She's just like us. And what did you expect me to do? Let him take her?"

Leaning her head to the side a little, Suina managed to see from where the voice originated. Nearby were two people a bit older than her. The first one was the boy she'd seen earlier, the one who'd saved her, complete with the same comforting, trustworthy vibe from before. The female near him, on the other hand, gave off a completely different vibe. She also showed signs of wounds, but all of them were minor, skin-deep, or narrow, as if whatever made them had used a million horseshoes just to get a hit. Her outfit seemed to be a simple, practical piece, easy to move in. Her glasses hid a gaze that seemed to stare into a person's soul, analyzing everything in sight. But what was most noticeable was the aura she had. Just by looking at her, you immediately got the sense that she would throw you to the sharks if she thought it was the smart choice. That your life was just another number. The thought alone was chilling to Suina. What was even more chilling was the fact that she was now trying to get her thrown out of...wherever this was.

"While unfortunate, if she was captured by her father, it would give us time to prepare better. While I'm sure he'd have nefarious intentions behind his actions."

"Well, congratulations on your moral victory. Unfortunately, she won't reap the benefits of your kindness. She's younger than the rest of us, and she'd have no idea what she's getting into. Besides, our remaining supplies are heavily strained as is. We can't afford the dead weight." That brought a slight, bitter smile to the boy's face.

"Man, you really don't pull your punches. Guess your brain's so big because your heart's the tradeoff."

The next words out of her mouth had very slight hints of anger and bitterness that hurt to hear.

"I have a heart. You of all people would know that better than anyone. I can simply...ignore it, to make the right call. And we *both* know my words here have merit." The boy seemed to grimace, but he didn't refute her words. When he spoke again, it was a black cocktail of frustration, sadness, and resignation.

"You and I both know he won't just use her as leverage. He'll try to use her to keep his group in check. He'll change her. She'll basically die if we send her back out there."

Those words successfully brought a brief pause to the girl's robotic behavior. For an instant, Suina thought she saw genuine sympathy inside that gaze, genuine sadness. But that instant was over as soon as it began, and the girl regained her composure as if it never left her. She took two small, short breaths. She closed her eyes for a second, before reopening them, shining with cold determination. When she spoke, it was heavily tempered, controlled and detached.

"And that...is unfortunate. I don't want that. Any more than you do. But that decision is one that must be made. We don't know enough about her for me to predict interactions. We don't know if she has any usefulness. It's just not worth it. I'm sorry."

"No, you're not." The boy half-yelled. For her part, the girl didn't flinch, even if her eyes betrayed a trace of pain.

"Yes, I am. I am sorry. But I'm not going to let that get us caught. That's the reason you wanted me here."

The boy's anger was tangible. The tension in the room was thick. Even so, after a second, the boy put his hands on a nearby table, clenching it hard, and said, "I... I'm sorry. I know. I... I just…I just wanted to help another one of us." The response he got was delayed but held a slightly softer tone.

"I know. I get it. But that simply isn't an option right now. We can't afford to just grab someone else."

The boy's scarred face now had a few tears of frustration going down them. Suina's first thought, weirdly enough, was something along the lines of, *maybe I should let them kick me out. I can't just drag them down.* She shook off that thought quickly though. Resolve flashed in her bright green eyes. An image of her mother flashed through her mind's eye. Guilt began to tug at her heart. *No. It's not a choice to throw away my life. If someone still needs it, this can't be where it ends.* And she still had questions, ones she needed answered. Her thoughts, and the silence, were cut off by the words, "Should we just do it?" Suina's blood turned cold in her veins. The boy's neck spun like a baseball to face the robotic being who said those words. Her face showed nothing. *Nothing.* It was as if she'd simply erased the traces of humanity she'd had before.

"It's arguably the more ethical choice. If we simply abandon her, let her father take her, it's basically the same. She'll be gone. Given your obvious feelings of guilt, wouldn't it be merciful to just end it here?"

The response was silence. For a second, Suina thought he simply ignored the statement. Then she heard the slow, hesitant but certain grabbing of a weapon. Her heart was a jackhammer. Yet the strike never came. Suina allowed herself a brief hope of escaping this situation before she heard yet more horrifying words:

"If you're hesitant, I can do it for you. It'll be quick. I promise."

Sensing things were not going in her favor, Suina figured now would be the perfect time to make it known she was up, and rapidly sprung halfway up. She contemplated trying sarcasm (that is what most kids her age used, right?), but it just wasn't her. It sounded too mean. In the end, she ended up producing something that sounded more like, "H-hi." Both people who had just been contemplating her death froze in their tracks. While the girl quickly pulled herself together, the boy's face quickly stained with guilt. He dropped the weapon, and rapidly walked towards her. He was about to start stammering a mixture of concerned questions, apologies and excuses when the spectacled girl simply said, "Well, this complicates things. Greetings. I would like to say it's a pleasure to meet you, but I feel it would ring hollow, given the circumstances." No kidding. Thinking quickly, Suina decided just doing her usual thing and being kind would be her best chance of survival.

"Um, y-yeah, I get it, I guess. Can I at least get your name?"

"With all due respect, I don't think it's a good idea to try and grow attached, given the situation. I hope you understand."

The cold tone those words were said with was still rather disturbing. It was clear to Suina that no matter what she felt personally, this girl would not relax and let her in. Even so, she had to try and make a friend…. or at least

"Fair enough, I guess. Are you...uh…"?

"Still going to kill you. Given the circumstances, it's a lot less likely. I doubt you would be willing to simply let me kill you, and I am still unsure of what you're capable of, which is the same reason why I was going to remove you *before* you woke up. Furthermore," she said, as her voice wavered slightly, "given the fact that you've woken up, my emotional state might affect my judgement, as I would find it...unpleasant to kill someone so young while they're aware of what's occurring. I might hesitate, or my aim might be off. I could end up turning what was meant to be instant slow and painful. So no, I no longer have any intention of your demise. And I know my ally *doesn't* want that. Do you, Everett?"

The boy whose name was Everett quickly shook his head. "No, I don't. I... *we* shouldn't have even considered it. Her life is hers alone. We have no right to make those choices for her. I... I'm sorry." Seeing the shame on the boy's face, Suina had the odd desire to comfort him despite everything, and she obliged.

"Don't be. I get where you were coming from. You just wanted to help. Thank you." Everett seemed to perk up a little.

"No prob. That guy was easy, anyway. He tried to follow me, but I lost him a while back. And besides, I couldn't just abandon you, now could I? Unlike *some* people..." He motioned to the girl behind him, who simply responded with,

29

"I don't regret my actions. I just wish I'd made sure to plan for your father. Dealing with him earlier would have made everything so much easier." A red flag. Suina immediately turned towards the girl.

"H-hold on! What do you mean by 'deal with him'?"

"Relax. I simply meant that I'd have planned a way to distract him. A small fire, perhaps."

"*What?*"

"I don't understand why you're so upset. It's not like it happened."

"No, it's just-I'm sorry, but I'm going to need some answers. "What do you know about my father? *How* do you know all this? Who *are* you guys? Why can you *punch people through trees?* Why do I keep having dreams about-"

"Slow down. I know you have questions, and you'll get some answers. But not right now. We don't know enough about you, yet."

"Then what *can* you tell me?"

"…well, Sophia? What can I tell her?" Sophia sighed.

"… it appears as though we can't just kick her out now. Tell her the basics. You can tell her about the war. The abilities. That should be enough for now." A slight smile crept across Everett's face. "Okay, I can work with that. So, what info do you want first?" The answer was quick.

"Tell me about the war."

"Oh? Not the one I expected you to pick."

"I-I keep having dreams about this girl…running through the forest…there's a bunch of fighting behind her…and-and bodies everywhere…"

"Oh, those? We all had 'em. Usually happens when you're getting closer to awakening your abilities. Mainly when you're thinking like them at the moment. Nothing big. Now that you're fully awakened, they should relax."

"That's…really it?"

"Pretty much. The power…it acts as a link between past and present, in some ways. Passed down. We don't really get it much yet though."

"Ok. Still…I want to know what was going on."

"Cool. So, you've heard of the war of two kingdoms, right?" Of course, she had. Everyone had. Even if most of the details had vanished, everyone knew the gist. "Two close kingdoms suddenly start fighting, millions die, then they suddenly just stop, and fuse into one kingdom."

"Yeah, suffice to say that war was *not* natural. Er, not entirely."

"Someone caused it?" Sophia cut in for a second.

"Calling it someone is overly generous. Some*thing* is far more accurate. But yes, it did. We don't have much info on how it was born, or what it is, but we do know what it *did.* The two kingdoms always had tension, and he ramped it up. Once the people disliked each other, he went for the kings. It took the worst parts of both kings- all their doubts, their biases, their grudges- and dragged them to the surface. *Decades* of friendship, gone in *days."*

"How is that possible?"

"We don't have much info on it. We believe your father holds some of whatever documents are left of what really happened. We intended to retrieve them while he was out looking for you, but he found out you were like us slightly faster than we expected, and his plans changed. Now we still must find a way to retrieve them, to learn more about them. It's important."

"Why? I mean, it's okay to want to learn more, but why is it so important right now?"

"...because they're coming back." A chill ran down Suina's spine.

"H-how would you know that?"

"Sorry, that's something I need to know right now. If we can get those documents, though...I'll be more willing to reveal what I know. That's fair."

"Okay, then. We...we can discuss that later, but I still have some questions about some things. You mentioned our abilities. Where'd they come from?" Everett jumped in.

"An excellent question...that we have no answer for. I mean, we know our ancestors had them, and they passed it down, but we don't know how *they* got 'em, or at least, we don't remember. Sorry. All we really know is that they're each based on something, a positive quality or trait."

"Positive quality? Then, that kid chasing me-"

"Believe it or not, people have nuance. You even saw it. The guy chasing you, he-he was perseverance personified. He never stopped, he never stayed down, he never gave up, and he kept going until his goal was changed. If I were to describe it as a game...imagine a character who stops taking damage at 1 HP, and has infinite stamina, until the goal's complete."

"...do you know what mine was?"

"We will figure it out, but not yet. Sorry."

"Oh...then what's yours?"

"Oh, I-"

"That's info that can be saved for later." Sophia butted in. "Once we get the files from your father's office."

Chapter Five

As they expected, the house was vacant when they arrived. As Sophia had predicted, all the guards were out-searching for Suina. The security cameras around the house were on, but unmoving. The person watching them must have gone with the rest of security. It was easy for Suina to walk to the door, use her key, and enter the place she'd never expected to be again. Immediately, she walked toward the area she knew the information would be: her father's office. As Suina's hand touched the door to the office yet again, she hesitated. The last time she'd opened this door, everything had gone wrong. Her entire life had changed forever. She couldn't help but wonder if she was making another mistake. If she'd regret coming back. She thought about the two people looking around, the ones who were hiding everything. She couldn't trust them any more than her father. Maybe she'd been wasting her time. The thought was rejected as swiftly as it'd appeared. It didn't matter, at this point. She was in too deep to quit, with a great push the doors flew open. As Suina stepped into the room, she noticed a pale woman, head buried in her hands on the nearby desk. She heard faint weeping from her and recognized the voice of her mother. She seemed to be talking to herself.

"I should have told her. I should have *known*. He burnt it all. He knew she was connected to-"

"-to…what, mom?"

Her mother froze. Looking up, she saw the face of her daughter for what felt like the first time in a decade. A daughter she'd been led to believe was dead. "S-Suina? Y-you're-" She was interrupted by her daughter rushing towards her, arms outstretched. Tears in her eyes, she accepted Suina's embrace.

"Oh, thank God. I thought I'd lost you." Releasing her hold, Suina looked her mother square in the eyes, a slight smile on her face and eyes wet with tears.

"I-I'm sorry I scared you like that…it's nice seeing you, mom." Shaking her head for a second, she focused back on what her mother was discussing.

"Mom…what should you have told me?" A sigh.

"I should have played a more active role in your life. I should have tried to do more for you, tried to protect you. I'm-I'm sorry." Countless emotions went through Suina's head.

"We-we can discuss all this later. But I need you to tell me what you should have told me."

"While you were gone, I looked through your father's documents. He…he left them on his desk. I had been trying to…to get something back, something he'd taken."

"What was it?"

"Some drawings, some writing about an ancestor of yours. They…they had been passed down the family, and he-he…I saw the burnt papers near the fireplace. I could read a little of what was left. Connect the dots." Her mom was clearly disturbed by the destruction of the papers. Suina had to feel for her a little but ignored it. She couldn't afford to lose focus.

"What did it say?"

"My-*your* ancestor…she wasn't like your father. She dedicated her life to helping people, to making a difference in the world. And that colored every aspect of her life. She even participated in the war…I…I'd thought as a medic. But, reading the journal…I…I found something. The-the writer, they-they mentioned a girl who-who could make shields, who protected people from battles. They asked her for her name, and she said her name was Kina, the same as our ancestor. I figured it couldn't be a coincidence. Your father probably had no idea. He just knew she was against everything he stood for…everything he became. He wouldn't let me keep a reminder that the person he'd turned into was against everything my family believed in." As she said this, her voice shook a little with restrained emotion.

"Mom…"

"I…I'm fine. Your father…he never was the best man. He was self-centered, a bit greedy. But he had moments of genuine love. Real compassion. I thought I could bring out that part of him…but he got worse. It

36

was as if…he'd decided everything was second to his desires, his ambitions. Including me."

"Mom…"

"…I'm sorry for laying all this on you. Suina, I have a question for you. Is…is the story true? Are you…are we like her?"

Suina hesitated, before nodding. Her mother's face took an odd tone. She seemed lighter than she had since Suina entered the door.

"I'm…glad to hear she passed something down. Something from our past. Something to remember her by. How…how did you learn you had it?"

She contemplated whether she should tell her mother everything, how her father had tried to kill her. She decided she couldn't do it.

"A long story. I'll tell you more when we have time, someday. Look, mom. I'm glad to see you, really, but I…I can't stay. I have some things I need to do, some things to find out." Her mom's smile fell clear off her face. Her disappointment was palpable.

"Oh…I understand. I assume you came here for the documents?" Suina could barely look her mother in the eye as she nodded.

"…yeah. The people I came with need them more than he does."

"That's probably true. But the question is, do you *trust* them with it more than him?" The question gave her pause for a moment before she responded:

"I trust they'll give me the answers I wanted. That'll do for now." The mom's frown grew.

"…I understand. I wish I could go with you. I could protect you, makeup for all the time I missed. I care about you." Suina couldn't help but wish the same. Even so…

"Me too, mom. But that's not for now. Someday. I promise. We can just…talk." As she was conversing with her mother on times far past and the future of their relationship, she heard yelling and gunfire outside. Her father's guards must have returned. The phone Sophia gave her roared to life.

"Suina, get out of there! A bunch of guards are about to burst into the place, they're gonna search his office any second!" Grabbing the papers, Suina prepared to leave, but before doing so, she turned again to her mother.

"I got my gift from you. If I can do it, so can you. Don't give up." The words slightly perked her up.

"I hope you find the answers you're looking for, Suina. And…I hope you find happiness, no matter what." With a smile at that last comment, Suina jumped out the broken window, but immediately found herself staring down the business end of at least half a dozen barrels, to her mother's horror.

"Wh-what are you doing?! Put those down!" The guards didn't seem to want to oblige and appeared to take the woman's request humorously.

"Sorry, *ma'am,* but your husband wants her captured, by any means necessary, even if that means things have to get...uncomfortable." Suina looked around, trying to find an angle to run from, but the guards weren't having it.

"You try it, I'll shoot. He needs you alive, not unharmed." Finally, Suina seemed to see a way to escape. She snuck her way out of the circle, almost escaping before she slipped and tumbled. The commenting guard came to her, head down. They appeared to be annoyed at her attempt.

"Why couldn't you just play nice and behave?" With that, they aimed the barrel at her and fired. She flinched...before noticing a dull green dome shatter in front of her, bullet, and all. She hadn't been the one to summon it. Panting from behind the broken window, shock apparent, was her mother. The guards were utterly stunned. However, the most they could get out was a "Wha-" before the other two teenagers showed up, looking a tad tired. The guards aimed their guns at Everett, only to be shocked when he tore them like tissue paper. After that, they attempted to flee, only to be picked off by Sophia, moving like a ninja in the night. As more began to arrive, Everett grabbed Suina's arm with a smile and said, "I'd definitely say you earned your answers. C'mon, let's book it before more arrive." As they ran into the forest, Suina saw her father at the front of the office, watching, and her blood ran cold. She thought of her mom, the person like her. The one she'd just left behind with *him.* However, he didn't even acknowledge her mother. Instead, he found her eyes as she ran off, and stared straight into her soul as she vanished into the night.

Chapter Six

The man frowned as he looked at the scene unfolding in front of him. As the child he once called his daughter ran off into the night. It was all he could do to contain the immense fury he felt from every cell. He stared at the guards, the ones who had fired on Suina. He grew mildly annoyed as he wondered if all his guards were so willing to blatantly disobey him. He'd have to make an example out of them later. Now, however, he turned to his wife. It had been a while since he'd seen her like this. She had become more and more reclusive over the years, as it had become more and more apparent that for all the benefits that came with the marriage, some of the more minor aspects of the deal like "love" and "allies" had been found to be lacking. The slightest pang of guilt assaulted the man's heart. He genuinely *did* want her to enjoy herself as his wife, even if only to keep her out of his hair and out of his plans. He'd originally married her only because she was attractive, and she was a member of the more "middle class" members of society, a boon for his awful P.R. He knew that. Despite that, he'd still hoped he could at least manage to salvage what little remained of their marriage. He wasn't sure what it was that made him want this. Was it love? Desire? All that mattered was that he wished for it to work. However, it seemed as though that was simply not to be. He looked again at his wife, who had started staring face down when he entered the room.

The instant he read that soldier's journal for the first time, the instant he'd read that name, the name whose legacy he thought he'd burnt to ash, he knew that his wife was more special than he'd originally believed. Yet another reason to have her. He had planned to test his theory after he'd returned with their daughter, but fate had something different planned for him. With a slight sigh, he finally began to talk. His voice was slow, tranquil, and polite, yet every word had an inferno of anger hidden deep inside.

"You read my documents; I see. That is not your fault. I should never have tempted you by leaving them unlocked. What *is,* however, your fault is our daughter's escape. You could have stalled her, convinced her to stay. Instead, you betrayed me. You let her go." Surprisingly, his wife didn't back down, like she usually did when she offended him somehow. She was shaking like a leaf, but her eyes betrayed a shockingly strong mix of anger and sadness.

"Yes, I let her go. She found me in here as I was looking for something. The documents on my ancestor. The ones you *burned."*

"…I didn't want to have to destroy them. I know how much they meant to you."

"Yet up in flames they went."

"I…I had feared our daughter's nightmares were somehow connected to your family heritage. I didn't want her to find information painting me in a bad light."

"H-how…how could you be so-"

"Selfish? Cruel? Evil? I've been called worse, dear, so please just say your piece so we can get this over with." The mother's face, previously white as a sheet, had practically turned red with fury.

"Well, since you requested it, *dear,* where should I even begin? This loveless excuse for a marriage you've got me trapped in. The hundreds of people who hate *me* for *your* crimes. The fact that you have secrets you felt were bad enough to *kill your daughter over,* the fact you *burned* centuries-old family artifacts because they made you *look bad,* hiding the fact that apparently, our daughter has *powers* stemming back *centuries,* to name *a few* of the things 'on my chest.' You've failed me *and* our daughter, in too many ways to count. All you've done, all you've *ever done,* is look out for yourself."

"That's interesting for *you* to say, the one who abandoned her daughter because she couldn't accept the reality of the situation. I may have failed, but you didn't even *try.* Unlike you, I've worked *tirelessly* for this family. Everything I've done is for us. To make sure we have the right leverage on the right people. All the information, the secrecy, it's all been to protect us, make sure we're safe. Our family, our *future."*

"A future you tried to rob from our daughter, who, I should note, has gained *nothing* from you. You justify your actions by using her, but she's never wanted *anything* you gave her. All she wanted was your *love,* and you *failed* her. Everything- her kind nature, her curiosity, her *abilities*-all come from *me."* As soon as she said the words, she froze. The dad instantly picked up on her slip.

"You're right. Her abilities *did* come from you. It's genuinely shocking they never materialized for you." The mom was flustered by his statement, caught off-guard. She tried to cover her error with genuine anger.

"I never had the chance. I was always stuck here, to avoid the mobs outside, or the enemies you made. I was robbed of that opportunity."

"And yet, looking back, it's really odd that Suina was even able to make that shield. As I walked in, she had just fallen attempting to run, and the moment she turned around, those guards opened fire. She barely had time to notice they'd fired, let alone react to it. So, I have to wonder…if she didn't make that shield…*who did?"*

Chapter Seven

Suina and company stumbled back into the base, putting their pilfered documents on the table before flopping into various chairs around. Even Sophia seemed to relax a bit, a slight smile on her face.

"That was a total success, I'd say. We got quite a bit of info from that trip, made it out with minimum injuries, and potentially have an ally still on the inside. Overall, not bad for a day's work." Suina immediately pounced on this.

"So, since I fulfilled my end of the bargain, doesn't that mean you have some answers to give me?" Everett's smile grew a little at this.

"Well, we *did* have a deal…and you do seem to have done your part here…I'd say you earned some answers to the questions from earlier. Wouldn't you, *Sophia?*" The way in which he commented was almost teasing, as though he *wanted* her to be annoyed. For her part, she didn't seem to be. She simply stated, "Truthfully, I'd rather not reveal so much so soon, but…I acknowledge your effort in completing the deal, not to mention the several other positives that came out of this affair." The small smile she had grew a little.

"You're entitled to the information you worked so hard for. Tell us what you want to know, if it's reasonable and I can tell you, I will." Suina instantly knew the first question she wanted to ask.

"What's *your* ability?" Sophia let out an audible sigh of mild frustration at this question.

"I had a feeling you'd ask a question like that. It's…complicated to explain, and I'm hesitant to explain it so soon to you, but to give you the bare basics…I can see the logical result of things."

"Oh, c'mon. You can at least afford to clarify a little."

"Tell you what. I promise to clarify everything, in detail. Soon. I just need a little time to figure out the right wording. Fair enough?" Suina had her reservations but nodded after a second of contemplation.

"Fair enough, but I expect you to keep your word."

"It makes no sense to lie about this."

"So, if it *did,* you'd have just lied?"

"This question has no positive outcome. Either I say no, and you assume I'm lying, or I say yes, and you start questioning things. Just don't overthink it." That wasn't an answer, but Suina still let it go.

"Fine. Are you at least going to fill me in on how his power works?"

"Everett? Oh, that's not really a major concern of mine at this point. He can tell you all about it, while I read the documents you stole from your father." Everett's smile grew even wider.

"*Finally.* Okay, so you've seen *part* of my power already." She thought back to him punching that

46

attacker straight through a tree and bending the guns of the guards like taffy.

"Yeah, you're strong. *Very strong!*" A slight chuckle.

"Depends. My power is based on my courage. I start strong, and get stronger and tougher when I go into a fight I'd lose otherwise, or if I'm scared, but fight anyway. I gotta admit, seeing a couple of dozen guys with rifles charging at you is a bit scary. Even with my power, it was a close call. A few lucky shots, and who knows?"

"And the guy who was after me?"

"That guy never stopped fighting and could shrug off my hits. He could have fought forever if he had to. I went into that with the sole purpose of getting you out of there, even if I had to fight someone I knew I couldn't beat."

"Huh. It's a lot more complicated than I thought."

"Yeah, but I make it work, as you saw out there."

"So, what would happen if you fought someone you knew you could beat?"

"...I actually don't know. I've never tried it. I'd probably just be a really strong guy." As the two were discussing Everett's ability, Sophia was reading the documents they received. With each one, her face grew grimmer. She seemed to be murmuring to herself about it all "making sense in the worst ways." She began to realize the scope of what they were dealing with. Suina seemed to notice and walked over to check on her.

"Hey, are you-"

"I'm fine. I just began to get a grasp of what exactly caused all this. You asked how I knew it was coming back, right? The thing that started the war?" A nod. "Well, these documents explain everything. A lot of it's disconnected, but together...we know how it was made, and why. Someone was meddling with a power they couldn't even hope to understand, and it backfired. Badly."

"Why would my father have these?"

"My guess? He wanted leverage on someone who knows this stuff's more than rumors. The same reason he wanted you when he found out you were special. He was worried that people from higher up would get in his way, and he wanted a deterrent, something to make them pause before making that decision." The disgust in that moment that Suina had for her father, for being willing to kill her to keep his leverage, was unimaginable. Sophia noted her reaction and commented.

"I don't suggest you blame your father entirely. He wasn't the mastermind behind this. As awful a person as he may be, someone pushed him towards this." Well, that was a shock.

"How do you know?"

"We've watched your father. He's changed. He never was a saint, but he used to be better...until a mysterious man in all black started coming around. A man whose description matches that of the person who started the conflict of kingdoms. And their name is-" *Suina.*

"The reason we knew he returned was that-" *Suina, can you hear me?* "He's been nudging on your father to make things worse so he can-" *Please help me.* "The last time we saw him-"

"Hold on, do you guys hear something?"

"No, what is it?"

"I think…" *Please help me.* "I think it's my mother. I think my father is hurting her."

"How do you know that?"

"I-I think I *heard* her. Talking to me." Everett and Sophia looked at each other, then back at Suina, concern in their eyes.

"It's probably just a mixture of concern for her and exhaustion. You've had a stressful day; you should relax and rest. If it really bothers you that much, we can look into it later." Suina was still hesitant. "It-it just-"

"We'll look into it while you rest. Let it go for now." Reluctantly, Suina let herself doze off. She opened her blurred eyes again to find herself in a white room, staring at a body laying secured on a gurney, surrounded by half a dozen men in what appeared to be hazmat suits. She heard a whimper originate from the limp body lying on the gurney.

Looking at the scene, she couldn't help but feel as though she recognized one of the men nearby.

Suddenly, she remembered the document she'd read, the one describing an argument with the king. He was a mirror image of the king's advisor, the one described in the documents from so long ago. From what she was hearing, she eventually realized he was her father's chief scientist, with as few scruples as the man before him. He ordered around scientists nearby, requesting a needle and some gauze, before turning back to the body on the table. As Suina looked closer, to see more of what was happening, she made the mistake of looking at the person's face. As soon as she did, all the color drained from her face, all the air vanished from her lungs. Paralyzed with utter horror, she gazed upon the pained face of her mother.

"Draw another three vials of blood from her," the chief scientist said.

"Along with the ones we took from our boss's newest asset, it should be enough to easily experiment with. And hook her up to a saline solution immediately. The last thing we want to do is kill her." Suina's mother groaned in pain as more blood was extracted from her. Suina's eyes were wet with tears as she watched, unable to do anything to aid her. All she could do was listen as one of the scientists asked, "Should we cut her hair off? It'd yield more D.N.A."

"Most of it. Our boss would not be pleased if we were excessive. Use the laser cutter. Lowest setting. We do want to be precise." A pained whimper continued in the air as the laser sliced slightly into the scalp of the body on the table, cutting the hair at the shaft. Suina's eyes were blurred with tears as she watched the pure, unfathomable evil these men had inflicted upon her mother without batting an eye. She couldn't help but feel a cold, bitter hatred creeping over her heart. She despised the beings who could treat another person like this, despised her *father* for allowing this to happen, for being so blinded by selfishness. But most of all, she was angry at *herself.* She should have known. The instant her mother helped her, the instant she saw her father, she should have done something. *Anything.* But she didn't. She *left her. This was her fault.* At that moment, clouded by rage, she could have sworn she heard someone reaching out to her. *Encouraging* her hatred. Telling her to burn it all down. Images of her father's mansion in flames swirled through her mind. She choked down these feelings, that black abyss of emotion dragging her down. She forced herself to calm down, her breathing too slow. This rage, this hatred…it wouldn't save her mother. Her eyes grew wetter. But what *would?* She had a hunch. It terrified her. But she knew it would work. If she…if she went back to her father…if she gave herself up…he'd not need her mother anymore. He'd let her go. He'd use her instead. The idea was horrifying. She had no idea what he'd do to her, make *her* do. And yet…if she could save her mother…if she could keep the parent who'd shown her even a semblance of love…she'd do it in a heartbeat. That thought, that one selfless loving desire, filled her with an energy unmatched. As she focused on it, on that one loving feeling, her mother briefly opened her eyes. And for an instant, the world turned pure white. She blinked, and in front of her was her mother, as she had been before. The needle marks on her arms, the singe marks on part of her scalp, it had all vanished. She looked as if years of stress had vanished from her, and her eyes possessed a resolve she'd lacked for years. She thought about what Everett had said, back in the beginning. *The power...it acts as a link between past and present, in some ways.* This was what he'd meant. It had been more complex than they'd even realized. The woman who was her mother was proof of that. With a smile, she walked up to her daughter, face stern, but loving.

"I know what you're thinking. I appreciate it. So, *so* much. But I can't let you."

"What do you mean? I can't leave you there!"

"I don't want you to. But this isn't what I meant when I asked you to save me. I would never ask you to do that."

"But-but you're...you're..." Tears began to fill her eyes again. For her part, her mom barely hesitated.

"I called for you in a moment of weakness. I've gotten my head together a bit. I...I don't matter here. Not in the long run. You're the one who he really wants. If I'm here, I keep him from looking for you too hard. I...I haven't...I haven't been that good of a mother up until now. I used to be better, a long time ago. But I…I let everything change me. I was weak. When things got difficult, I shut myself away, abandoned you, and I will never forgive myself for that."

"M-mom, I…" For once, her mother seemed to have a genuine smile on her face, even if it looked a tad strained.

"I was so, so selfish, Suina. I'm so sorry for that. But for the first time in years, I'm thinking of someone besides myself, of someone I truly *care* about. Staying here and buying you some time is the absolute least I can do."

"B-but Mom…"

"I know it'll hurt, you and me alike. But I know that someday, you'll change things. Someday, you'll be back for me. And on that day, we'll meet again. When you're ready."

"But how will I know when that is? I want to help you now!"

"You'll know, I promise. You'll know. This, this connection we share, you created that. You introduced me to this, gave me this opportunity to keep you safe. This is just a sign that you're stronger than you know. I read the documents your father had. If what they say is true...you have more potential than you can ever imagine. That loving heart, that selfless spirit…there's no limit to what you can do. You, or the others."

"I love you, mom."

"I love you, too. Now, wake up. You have more important things to do than chat with me. Oh, but before you do..." Her mother's eyes closed. Ideas, information entered Suina's head, words about the powers shown long ago, images of the potential she could achieve.

"I found the concept for most of these in the journal. A lot of them are just guessing from what was there, and you'll need to learn how to use them, but..." A slight chuckle, filled with hints of bitterness.

"Consider it a late birthday present." The white world they were in began to fade away, and the last words Suina heard were, "Stay safe."

When Suina woke up, tears were in her eyes. Her heart ached with pain, unlike anything she could have imagined. But she forced herself to ignore it. That wouldn't help anyone. She knew what she had to do. She had to get stronger. She had to save her mother. As she looked in the mirror, she noticed she'd changed. Her eyes, once a dull green, now were bright as the sun. She saw herself covered in a thin green armor, from head to toe, a shield against things to come. She balled her fist, and it closed easily as if it was skin. She thought about the experience she'd just had, of the many possibilities open to her. She'd need to learn them all to achieve her goals now. She knew it would probably be a good idea to tell the others all that she'd learned...all that she'd seen. She began to walk to where she knew Sophia's room was, noticing the sound of conversation nearby. As she was about to enter, she heard Everett say, "we can't hide the others from her. We have to fill her in. Especially if what she said is true. At least tell her what you found out about the kid from earlier."

"She was impressive today, that much I admit. She also got us valuable information that we can use to plan. I'm grateful to her. But I'm not willing to reveal so much to her so soon, especially not with her family. She doesn't need to know about the others like us we found yet. Not their names, not their powers, anything."

"Fair enough. But speaking of her family, you figure out if her mom's okay?"

"We didn't have the time, so I used my power. I lack a lot of info on her, but I believe she's been captured and experimented on."

"That's…rough. Do we tell her? Or do anything?"

"We don't need her distracted, especially if we plan on giving some more information. On buying more time. Her mother can wait. We'll simply hold onto what we know for now."

"No." Suina finally stepped in, unable to simply watch anymore. The two plotters noticed her, cloaked in her thin green coat. Her eyes had a certain fury to them that was shocking to see.

"No. I'm tired of only getting little bits and pieces of the story. My father is attempting to find others like us, for a plan I know *nothing* of. I just found out my mother's being used as an experiment, so I don't have to be. All you two have done is hide things from me, use me to get things in exchange for scraps of the story. I am in a terrible mood right now and I'm *done* waiting for you two to give me the info I need. So, here's what's going to happen. You're going to tell me about the others like us. You're going to tell me what you found out about the kid from earlier. *You're going to tell me everything."*

About the Author

"Danny Williams is the *author of The Legacy Awakens, the first book in a series that he began writing while still a student in high school. Having overcome many adversities including Autism, Type I Diabetes, and the death of his father and best friend, Danny is an advocate for the power of positive thoughts and emotions. He creatively employs virtue as a source of power for his budding heroes while cleverly crafting the detriments of negative energy into the book's villain. Danny both entertains and educates as he transports readers to a place where evil develops and thrives from vile sentiments and virtues invest the most common and unsuspecting with power beyond their imagination.*

You can visit him online at https:// **thelegacyawakensseries.godaddysites.com**